SPRINGTIME TALES

Designed and Illustrated by
Ann Patrice Wilson

Written and Adapted by
Nan Roloff and Deborah Apy

Table of Contents

The Coming of Spring

by Nan Roloff

Spring is a maiden,
   Gentle and fair
    With tresses that shimmer
    Like rays of the sun.

She drifts in on a breeze
   To caress the bare branches
   And awaken the leaves—
    Now Spring has begun!

The beasts of the forest
   All gather to greet her,
   To feed from her hand
      And to gaze at her face,

And even the unicorn,
   Shyest of creatures,
   Comes forward to meet her
      From his hiding place.

Then hour upon hour
   She weaves fragrant flowers
   Into his soft mane
     By a clear waterfall,

For beautiful Springtime
   Can take coldest Winter
   And the wildest of creatures
     And make friends of them all.

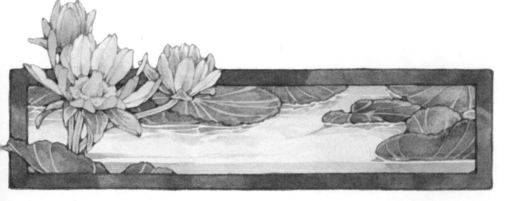

SPRING FEVER

by Deborah Apy

The sun shone. The leaves fluttered. The birds sang . . . "cheep, peep, tweet!" Roy Raccoon rolled out of his bed and peeked out the window. "Ahh . . . spring," he sighed happily.

One-two . . . one-two . . . one-two . . . he touched his toes ten times. He did ten pushups. Then he ran around his room very fast, ten times. When he stopped, he splashed cold water all over himself. "Brrrrr!" he wiggled his whiskers and stretched his nose.

Roy Raccoon hurried out the door onto his branch. A sign that said "R. Raccoon" hung from the tree trunk. Roy dusted off the sign with his

feather duster. He edged it over a bit so the sun shown on each letter. "Just right," hummed Roy.

"What's up there, Roy?"

Roy looked down and saw Willie Weasel. Willie's nose was scrunched up. His eyes squinted in the sunshine. Willie always acted so sneaky, Roy thought. But today he felt too good to care about that.

"Just feelin' good," Roy said.

"'Bout what?"

"Spring, Willie! It's spring."

"Yeah . . . a day in spring. So what's the big deal?"

"The big deal? Everything. Kites. Kites and flying them. Marbles. And mud puddles. And jump rope. And no jackets and mittens. And daisies . . . and playing tag . . . and . . ."

"Hmmmph," sniffed Willie. "You probably even like spring cleaning."

Roy watched Willie patter off. He sighed. It was true. He did like spring cleaning. It made everything so nice and fresh. Oh, well. Today Roy was not going to let Willie make him feel dumb. He went inside, climbed to his loft, and got his kite. Then he found his bag of marbles. Roy started to whistle.

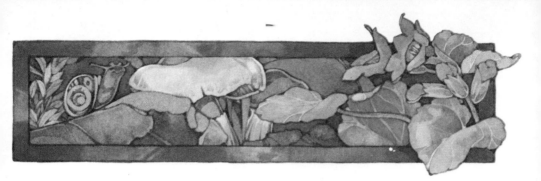

Bam! Bam! Bam! Something was hitting his door.

"Wha . . . ?" said Roy, falling flat on his tail
as he opened the door. Through the doorway burst
Oshua Squirrel, scattering Roy and his marbles
all over the place. Oshua was Roy's best friend.

"Roy! You should be in bed!" Oshua pushed
Roy onto his pillow.

"Wrap this around you!" Oshua threw a blanket
on his friend.

"Hold this to your head!" Oshua slapped a cold
washcloth to Roy's forehead and placed Roy's
paw on top of it.

"Now I'll make some tea." Oshua ran nervously
to the stove.

"But why, Osh?"

Oshua stared at his friend. "'Cause you're sick."

"Who said I was sick?"

"Willie. He said you had a gross case of spring fever."

"Oshua . . ."

"Yeah?"

"I'm not sick."

"You're not?"

"No. I just like spring. It makes me happy."

"Oh . . ." Oshua stared at his toes. His face got red. "That Willie's such a bother."

"Oh, Willie doesn't bother me," said Roy.

"He doesn't?"

"No. Willie just made me think of the best thing there is about spring."

"He did?"

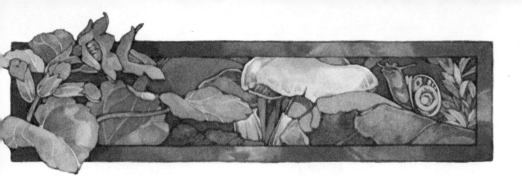

"The best thing about spring," said Roy, "is having a friend like you to share it with."

Oshua smiled. His face stopped being red. Oshua and Roy went outside. They flew Roy's kite. They played marbles. They jumped rope. It was a beautiful day.

The End

Fairy Flowers
by Deborah Apy

What wondrous worlds there are when starry
    blossoms gleam
In the late, night sky. A shimmering queen,
Of fairy stock, tarries among the flowers
Exchanging sweet report of long, enchanted hours.
With sudden dawn all vanishes, leaving not a trace
Except the dew that drifts above a field of grace.

NICOLA'S GRAPES

A Sicilian Folk Tale
adapted by Deborah Apy

Long, long ago there lived a small boy named Nicola who lived with his five brothers and six sisters and his mama and papa in a little house on an old farm. Nicola's family had no money, not even enough for seed to plant the fields, and though they wished to work there seemed to be no way for them to make a living. All they had was an arbor of grapes at the back of their house, and there, every spring, the luscious, purple fruit ripened on the vine.

One warm day Nicola's mother said to him, "Nicola, it is time to take the grapes to market.

Go now, and pick them, and see that you get a
good price for them, as they are all we have."

"Yes, Mama," said Nicola, and soon the ragged
boy was trudging down the dusty road, a basket
of grapes slung over his arm.

Now Nicola was a very small boy and although
his grapes were large and meaty, he was so small
that no one noticed him in the hustle and bustle
and commotion of all the sellers and buyers. As
the day lengthened, Nicola grew tired and very
discouraged. He was hungry. He thought about
eating the grapes, but then he remembered his
mama's words, and tried to put his hunger out
of his mind.

Then from the midst of the crowd an old and
ugly woman came hobbling towards him. Her skin

was wrinkled and covered with many warts, but
her eyes seemed kind and soft. "Will you give me
just a few grapes?" she asked weakly. "I have no
money and I am so very hungry."

Nicola looked at the old, skinny woman and she
did indeed seem very hungry, and as forlorn as
he. Without even thinking he handed her the
choicest grapes he had. The woman ate them
thankfully, and with each grape she swallowed
she grew younger and younger, and her clothes
more and more beautiful, until soon her entire
appearance was as kind and soft as her eyes
had first been.

Nicola gazed in astonishment at the young girl
before him. Gently she said, "Now, Nicola, take
the rest of the grapes back to your father's field

and plant them there, one at a time."

Nicola sprang to his feet and raced home down the dusty road, sure this woman was either a fairy or a witch, and not wanting to displease her, whichever she was. As she had told him, he carefully planted each grape. Then he turned to pick up his basket and go home to his family. He knew they would be angry and disappointed with him for he had neither grapes nor money now. What would they do?

But when Nicola lifted his basket it was very heavy. He lifted the cloth and gasped. There, for each grape the woman had eaten, lay a gleaming gold piece!

Nicola's feet fairly flew across the fields as he raced home. Now his family would have enough money for seed . . . and probably a plow and even an ox to pull it. Nicola's mama was pleased and proud and hugged her son for a long time. Nicola's papa was pleased and proud and beamed at his son and told him it was a manly thing he had done. Nicola's brothers and sisters laughed and smiled and patted him on the back, and his youngest sister asked, "But why did the woman tell you to

plant the other grapes?"

Nicola and his mama and his papa and all his brothers and sisters went back to his father's field. There, for each grape he had planted, bloomed a bright purple crocus. And for all the years there-after, until Nicola himself was an old man with many grandchildren, the bright showy flowers bloomed in increasing numbers each spring. And the family prospered in wealth and happiness, and was grateful for all they had received since that spring day when Nicola had shared his grapes with an old, ugly woman.

The End

The Animal's Picnic
by Deborah Apy

The billy goat brought artichokes,
The cat brought a tomato,
The dog, he was a silly bloke,
He dug up a potato.
The fat, old sow, she milked the cow
And made herself some cheese;
While sheep and hens came there and then
With oranges to squeeze.

'Twas avocados the river otter
Brought from California.
They smelled so nice the local mice
Said, "Please, sir, can we join ya'?"
The geese brought bran, the bull had jam,
The snails had macaroni;
And deviled eggs and lemonade
Came with the spotted pony.

The sun shone high up in the sky
When first they started lunching.
It slid into afternoon
But still they kept on munching.
And even when the moon did rise
They all were sitting tight,
And said, "This is so fine I think
We'll just stay here all night!"

The Easter Rabbit

by Deborah Apy

Once there was a family who lived in an old
stone house with a large garden behind it. One
part of the garden was filled with lovely, simple
flowers . . . pansies, petunias, daisies, and mums.
In the other part of the garden were vegetables,
and already in the early spring lettuce, spinach,
and radishes could be seen poking their stems up
through the ground. The children of the family
would come out to play in the garden in the afternoons, and they always brought their pet rabbit
with them. He was white with soft, broad floppy
ears. The rabbit would crouch very still, and then
take a big leap towards the vegetables. Then the

children would laugh and pick him some lettuce and feed him and stroke his fine, silky back and say what a beautiful rabbit he was. They were all very happy.

But a day came when the family moved from their house in the country to a house in the city, and they could not take their rabbit with them. So the children took him to the garden where they had played for so many hours and said, "Dear little rabbit, you must make your home in the garden now. When you come to know the other wild rabbits, you will be happy. We will never forget you . . . we are so sad to leave you." They left the rabbit there.

"Well," thought the little rabbit. "This will be fine. I have always liked the garden so." He hopped under the lilac bush and looked around.

Then something jumped right next to his big, back foot. "What's that!" cried the startled rabbit.

"Hrrumph," croaked a bumpy toad. "Me. Who are you?"

"I'm the rabbit who used to live in the house. And now I've come to live in the garden," replied the rabbit.

"Well . . ." croaked the toad again, "you are a house rabbit. What do you know about living in the wild?"

"I can learn," said the rabbit timidly.

"Who will teach you?" asked the toad.

"Why, the other rabbits."

"I doubt it . . ." said the toad. "But we will see." And the toad hopped away.

"Gee," the rabbit thought. "I wonder why he said that? I am awfully hungry, and a little cold. I wish I'd meet some other rabbits."

But it wasn't until it started to get dark that the rabbit heard a thump, thump nearby. Then across the garden he saw two dark brown noses, and then four beady eyes.

"Hey! Hey!" cried the rabbit, but the eyes and

noses disappeared. "Darn . . ." he muttered. Then hop, hop . . . two brown rabbits stood there staring at him. "Who are you?" they asked.

"I'm the house rabbit. But now I live in the garden, so I'm the garden rabbit."

"Pretty funny looking for a rabbit," said the first wild rabbit. "Look at how thin and pale your fur is. Hmmmph."

"And your ears," said the other. "How did they get so floppy? Did you break them?" The two rabbits laughed.

"Don't laugh. I am a rabbit, just like you. I'm cold and hungry, too. Where do you get your clover and barley? And where do you sleep?"

"Clover and barley?" they laughed loudly. "Good luck! You get what you can find. And to

29

sleep you find a hole in the ground, or dig one, and sleep there. That's what you do."

"But I always sleep in my hutch . . ." the rabbit said, and then sighed as the two hopped away. They hadn't been much help. "I guess," he thought, "the toad was right." And he sighed again, only much louder this time.

The days went by and the little rabbit had made no friends. He didn't seem to be able to get along with the chipmunks and toads any better than he had with the wild rabbits. He was lonely, and his pretty white fur was all brown and muddy now. The poor little rabbit wasn't nearly as happy as he had thought he would be. In fact, he was very unhappy.

Then one day the wild rabbits came running

through the garden. "Hide! Hide!" they cried. "People are coming!" All the creatures ran and hid as fast as they could. The white rabbit hid, too. Crouched stone-still beneath a bush, he watched and listened carefully.

Tap, tap, tap came the sounds of footsteps on the stone path. Two children came laughing and skipping and running. They looked so happy and nice the rabbit almost hopped out from under the bush. But he was too shy.

All the wild creatures no longer came to the garden now that there were people back at the house, so the little rabbit was quite alone. Every day he would peer out from under his bush and watch the children. "How pretty they are," he would think, but still he couldn't bring himself to

come out. "I'm too ugly and dirty," he would sigh.

One morning, when the rabbit awoke, there was a strange looking egg close by, all purple and orange and yellow. Then tap, tap, tap! he heard the children running again, and he crouched very still. This time, though, the children slowed down and started looking all around them, in places they never used to look. "How peculiar," thought the little rabbit, and he crouched down even a little more.

Then crunch, a small shoe stopped by his very nose. The rabbit shook and shivered and shook and shivered as a hand pushed some leaves aside. "Oh dear, oh dear," quivered the rabbit. There was a light gasp, and a little girl crouched down, staring at the poor bedraggled creature.

Very gently, she put her hands around the rabbit's body, and very gently she put the rabbit into her basket. "Oh, you dear little thing," she murmured, and made nice noises to make the rabbit feel safe. Then she laid a coverlet over the rabbit and picked up her basket.

"My, Jill," a voice said, "is your basket so heavy already? Have you found so many eggs?"

The rabbit felt the basket sway ever so slightly back and forth . . . back and forth. Then the coverlet was raised. "Look," a happy voice said. "I've found an Easter bunny!"

From that day on, the rabbit lived with his new family. He slept in a hutch by the house, and in the afternoons, when the little girl came home from school, she took him to the garden and

picked lettuce for him. And then she would stroke his back and tell him how fine and beautiful he was, and the rabbit was very happy.

The End

The Snowdrop

by *Hans Christian Andersen*
adapted by Nan Roloff

Outside, the winter wind was harsh and the air was cold. But inside the flower's little house, tucked safely beneath the earth, all was cozy and warm.

Then one day the rain showered gently upon the earth. The drops soaked slowly into the soil and touched the little bulb, bringing a message from the world above. Not long after, a ray of sunshine warmed its way through the snow and knocked at the little flower's door.

"Come in," said the flower.

"Not yet," replied the sunshine. "I am still not

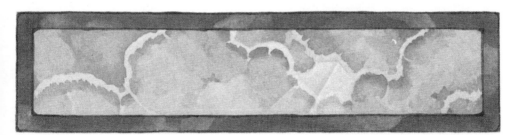

strong enough to open your door, but I'll be back
in summer!"

"And when will summer come?" asked the flower.
But summer was far away. Snow still blanketed
the earth and each night the rain that fell in
puddles was turned into ice.

"How long it takes," sighed the little flower
impatiently. "I'm tired of being all cooped up.
I want to get out and see the world. I want to stretch
and say 'Good morning' to the summer and to
the sun!"

With that the little flower stretched with all
its might inside its bulb house and broke through
the thin walls which the rain had softened and the
sun warmed. Through the earth and under the
snow, it grew, with a delicate white bud on its

green stalk. Its long narrow leaves reached up the stem and hugged the little bud to protect it. The snow was cold but sparse, so the light peeked through and the flower could tell the rays of sunshine were getting stronger.

"Welcome, little flower!" they sang; and the flower lifted its head through the freezing snow and into the world of sunshine. The rays hugged and kissed it so much it opened. The flower was as white as the snow and had fine green lines. It was so happy to be in the world, it hung its head with humility.

"Dear flower," sang the rays of sunshine. "You are so fresh and pure. You are the first and only flower that has come! We love you so! Your little white bell will ring that summer has arrived, that

the snow will melt, and the cold wind will fade away. We shall shine over all the earth and everything will become green. You will have lots of company! The daisies and lilacs will bloom, and then the roses will come. But you, little snowdrop, are the very first flower!"

What a pleasure all of this was! The little snowdrop felt quite spoiled by all the attention and felt that the air itself sang to it. How happily it basked in the sun's warm rays, dressed in its white dress with green ribbons. And it praised the coming of summer.

But summer was still a long way off. The clouds began to block out the sun and the wind blew cold as ever. "You have come too early!" cried the wind and clouds at the little flower. "We are still powerful and will make life hard for you.

You should have stayed in your house and not come out to parade in your fancy dress!"

Then the weather turned cold and dark and the sun disappeared. It was the kind of weather that normally would have frozen such a little flower. But the snowdrop was stronger than it realized, for it had felt the warm rays of sunshine and was sure in its heart that summer would come. So it stood there in its little white dress and braved the wind and snow, bending its head as the cold snowflakes fell all around it.

"You'll never make it," howled the wind. "First you will freeze, then you will wither. The sun rays have made a fool of you! You are a summer fool!"

"Summer fool," repeated the little flower in the

cold morning air.

"Summer fool!" squealed some little children who had just come into the garden and spied the little flower. They called it the same name as the wind, for that is what a snowdrop is called in Denmark.

"How beautiful it is! It is the very first flower of the year and the only one in the garden!" said a little girl as she stooped over the snowdrop. All the children gathered around the flower and kissed it, and to the snowdrop they were as warm and sweet as the sun rays. She was so happy she did not even mind waiting for summer a little longer! She would welcome the coming of spring!

The End